THE BRAVE LITTLE TAILOR

(Original Title: <u>Seven at One Blow</u>)

Retold by FREYA LITTLEDALE

Illustrated by LILLIAN HOBAN

SCHOLASTIC INC.

New York Toronto London Auckland Sydney

For Glenn and Lyssa
F. L.

ISBN 0-590-42797-0
Text copyright © 1976, 1990 by Freya Littledale.
Illustrations copyright © 1990 by Lillian Hoban.
All rights reserved. Published by Scholastic Inc.

12 11 10 9 8 7 6 5 4 3 2   0 1 2 3 4 5/9

Printed in the U.S.A.   23

First Scholastic printing, April 1990

Once upon a time, in the middle of summer,
a little tailor sat at a window
cutting some cloth.
Outside, he heard a woman call,
"Jam for sale! Who will buy my good, fresh jam?"

"I will!" shouted the little tailor.
And he bought some strawberry jam.

The little tailor spread the jam on a bun.
Then he saw flies coming after his jam.
"Buzz!" went the flies.

"Who asked you here?" said the little tailor.
"This jam is mine."

"Buzz! Buzz!" went the flies.

"Go away!" said the tailor.

"BUZZ! BUZZ! BUZZ!" went the flies.

"Now you're going to get it!"
cried the tailor. And WHAM!
He hit the flies with a broom.

He killed seven flies—
all at one blow!
He counted the flies:
"One, two, three, four,
five, six, seven!"

"What a great fellow I am!" said the tailor.
"The whole world should hear about this."

So he made a belt for himself.
On it he stitched in big letters:
SEVEN AT ONE BLOW.

The tailor tied the belt around his waist.
"Now I'm ready to tell the world," he said.

He put a small white cheese in his pocket.
Near his doorstep, he found a tiny bird
caught in a bush.
He put the bird in his pocket, too.
Then he set off down the road.

The road led to a mountain,
and he climbed all the way up.
A giant sat at the top.

"Hello, giant," said the little tailor.
"I'm on my way to tell the world
what a great fellow I am.
Would you like to come with me?"

"Ho! Ho! Ho!" laughed the giant.
"What's so great about you?
You're nothing but a little pipsqueak!"

"I may be little," said the tailor,
"but look!" And he pointed to his belt.

The giant read slowly,
"SEVEN...AT...ONE...BLOW."

The giant thought the little tailor had killed seven men.
Of course, he didn't know about the flies.

"Not bad," said the giant. "But can you do this?"
He picked up a big white stone and squeezed
until water dripped from it.

At once the little tailor took the cheese from his pocket
and squeezed until the water dripped from it.

"How about this?" asked the giant.
He picked up a stone and threw it so high
the tailor could hardly see it.

"Good throw," said the tailor,
"but that stone fell to the ground.
I'll throw one so high
it will never come down."

The tailor took the bird
from his pocket
and threw it in the air.
The bird flew up...up...
up in the sky
and was gone.

"Hmmmm!" said the giant.
"You are little,
but you do seem strong.
Can you help me carry
this big tree?"

"That's easy," said the tailor.
"You carry the trunk,
and I will carry the branches.
They're the heaviest part."

"All right," said the giant,
and he lifted the trunk onto his shoulder.

The tailor jumped up on the branches.
So the giant had to carry the tree
and the tailor, too.
It was a fine ride for the little tailor.
He whistled all the way.

But the giant grew very tired.
"Look out!" he called.
"I'm going to drop the tree!"

The tailor jumped to the ground
and pretended to lift the branches.
"What's the matter, giant?" he asked.
"Can't you carry a little tree like this?"

The giant was out of breath.
"If you're...so brave...and strong," he said,
"I dare you to spend the night
in my cave.
It's filled with giants."

"Why not?" said the little tailor.
And off they went.

Soon they came to the cave
where six giants sat around a fire.
Each one was eating half a cow.

"What a nice place you have here!" said the tailor.
"It's much bigger than mine."

"It's our home," said the giant.
"We're very happy here.
Now you must be tired.
Why don't you go to sleep
on this nice big bed?"

"Thank you," said the little tailor.
But the bed was much too big for him.
He got up
when the giants weren't looking,
and went to sleep
in a corner of the cave.

At midnight, the giants thought
the tailor must be sound asleep
in the bed.

So they took their clubs and smashed the bed to pieces. "There!" said the giants. "That's the end of the little fellow who can kill seven at one blow."

Early in the morning, the giants left the cave
and went into the forest.
Soon they heard someone whistling.
They looked down and saw the little tailor.

"He's supposed to be dead!" cried one giant.

"He must be a ghost!" cried another.

And all the giants ran away as fast as they could.

The little tailor went on his way.
He walked out of the forest,
and he kept on walking
until he came to the king's garden.

"This is a fine place to rest," he said.
And he lay down under a tree
and closed his eyes.

The king's men found
the tailor fast asleep.
They read the words on his belt:
SEVEN AT ONE BLOW.

"He must be very brave,"
one of the men said.
"Let's take him to the king."

So they woke the tailor
and took him to the king.

"What can I do for you?" the little tailor asked the king.

"There's a wild boar near a hut in my forest," said the king.
"It killed three of my men. If you catch the wild boar,
I promise you half my kingdom and my daughter for your wife."

The princess stood
beside her father.
She smiled at the little tailor.
And the little tailor
smiled at her.

"I'll do it!" said the tailor.
And he set off for the forest.

Near a hut, he saw the wild boar.
The boar looked very big and very wild,
and its teeth looked very sharp.

When the wild boar saw the little tailor,
it ran after him. It chased him right
into the hut.

The tailor jumped out of the window,
ran to the front, and locked the door.
The boar was trapped inside.

The tailor whistled a little tune
and went back to tell the king.

"I caught the wild boar," he said.
"Now may I have half the kingdom
and your daughter for my wife?"

"Not just yet," said the king.
"There's a unicorn in my forest.
It hurt five of my men with its horn.
If you catch the unicorn,
you shall have your reward."

"Very well," said the little tailor.
And he took a rope and an axe
and set off for the forest.

Soon he saw the unicorn,
and the unicorn saw him.
It was ready to attack.

The little tailor stood still
until the beast came close.
Then he stepped behind a tree.
The unicorn ran its horn
straight into the tree.
And there it stuck fast.

The little tailor tied the rope
around the unicorn's neck.
He freed the horn from the tree
with his axe.

Then he whistled a little tune
and took the unicorn to the king.
"Here it is," said the little tailor.
"Now I want my reward."

"I demand one more favor," said the king.
"There are two giants near the river.
They kill everyone they meet. Can you kill giants?"

"Of course I can," said the little tailor.
"I'm the fellow who killed seven at one blow."
And he set off for the river.

He found the giants under a tree.
They were fast asleep and snoring—
"ZZZ ZZZZZ ZZZ ZZZ ZZ!"

The tailor filled his pockets with stones.
He climbed quickly up the tree.
Then he dropped stones on one of the sleeping giants.

The giant woke up and pushed his friend.
"Why are you hitting me?" he asked.

"I didn't hit you. You must be dreaming."
And they both went back to sleep.

The little tailor dropped stones
on the second giant.

The giant woke up and shouted, "Don't hit me!"

"I didn't hit you!" said the first giant.
"Now you're the one who's dreaming."
And they both went back to sleep.

Then the tailor dropped
stones on both giants.
He threw them as hard
as he could.

The giants
woke up and began to fight.
They were so angry
they pulled up trees.
They hit each other
with the trees
until they both fell dead
on the ground.

The little tailor whistled a little tune
and went back to tell the king.
"I did it!" he said. "The giants are dead.
You can send your men to bury them.
Now will you keep your promise?"

"I will," said the king.

There was a great feast. The princess and the tailor were married. And the little tailor was made king of half the kingdom. He always wore his crown, and he always wore his belt with the words, SEVEN AT ONE BLOW.